Our Three Friends
Who Caught the Thieves?

Illustrated by J.-L. Macias S.

Pamela, Nancy and Daniel are so happy that their neighbor, Farmer Jackson, has promised to take them to a party in the meadow tomorrow. Pamela and Nancy are going to wear their best dresses. How nice of their neighbor to invite them!

The next morning everyone is ready on time. Mr. and Mrs. Jackson and their children have come to pick them up. "Good morning. Thank you for inviting us," says Pamela. "We are glad to have you with us," says Mr. Jackson. "Now come on everyone, let's get going—the party is waiting."

Everything at the party is so exciting for the three children, especially the little puppet theater. Candy and games are also part of the fun.

Daniel is very clever. He climbs to the top of the pole and wins . . . guess what . . . a beautiful live duck.

Nancy can't believe her eyes. She is actually riding on a merry-go-round, just like the ones she has seen so often in her picture books.

It's lunch time and everyone is very hungry. They discover a lovely spot at the foot of a tree and begin to eat. But before long a horseback rider arrives with bad news — some farms in the area have been robbed.

When our little friends arrive home they see an abandoned cart
in front of their house. The front door has been forced open. The
cart must belong to the thieves who have broken in. But where
are they now?

Everyone jumps out of the wagon. "They must be inside, busy stealing," says Daniel. "Don't be afraid," Pamela comforts Nancy. "The thieves won't take anything from us."

Suddenly muffled noises and groans are heard inside the house and everyone hurries past the smashed door to see what's happening. What a surprise! The table and chairs have been knocked over, the chest of drawers has been ransacked, a bag with some valuable objects has been left in the corner . . . and an angry big brown bear is looking up at two frightened burglars perched on top of a cupboard.

Everything ends happily. The policemen have taken the thieves away, and Nancy gives her friend the bear a big hug.

Published in the United States and simultaneously in Canada by Joshua Morris, Inc
431 Post Road East, Westport, CT.06880
Printed in Belgium